Praise for the Urgency Emergency! series

★"Top-notch medical care in an equally terrific early reader that will appeal to preschoolers, new readers of all ages, and anyone else who appreciates droll humor and an inventive plot."
—*Kirkus Reviews* starred review

★"New readers are in for a treat."—*Horn Book* starred review

"Archer's thickly painted illustrations exude personality and humor, and emerging readers will get a kick out of seeing the repercussions of a familiar story play out in an emergency room setting."
—*Publishers Weekly*

"There is plenty of sly humor in the text."—*School Library Journal*

"The folkloric connections broaden the use possibilities for libraries and classrooms, and the titles could inspire student writing or dramatic projects in a similar vein, while the medical situations are surprisingly educational."
—*Bulletin of the Center for Children's Books*, recommended

"Valuable lessons about overcoming fears and setting aside differences for others are emphasized."
—*Library Media Connection*

To the lovely Matt Hornsby

Library of Congress Cataloging-in-Publication
data is on file with the publisher.

Text and illustrations copyright © 2016 by Dosh Archer
Published in 2016 by Albert Whitman & Company
ISBN 978-0-8075-8349-4

Printed in China
10 9 8 7 6 5 4 3 2 1 LP 24 23 22 21 20 19 18 17 16 15

For more information about Albert Whitman & Company,
visit our web site at www.albertwhitman.com.

URGENCY EMERGENCY!

Baaad Sheep

Dosh Archer

Albert Whitman & Company
Chicago, Illinois

It was another busy day at City Hospital. Doctor Glenda was putting some pills into a bottle, and Nurse Percy was looking after Little Bo Peep.

She was very upset because
she had lost her sheep.

Just then the
ambulance arrived.

"Urgency Emergency!" cried the Pengamedics. "We have three sick sheep coming through!"

Old MacDonald the farmer was with the sheep. He was the one who had called the ambulance.

The sheep had sore tummies and were feeling very sick.
"Let me examine them!" said Doctor Glenda.

"It is just as I thought. Their tummies are sore and they feel very sick."

"Can you tell us
your names?" asked
Nurse Percy.

"Rocky," said Rocky.
"Enzo," said Enzo.
"Lulu," said Lulu.

"What made you all so sick?" asked Nurse Percy.

But the sheep would not say.
  "We need to know what we are
dealing with," said Doctor Glenda.
"Bring me my special
Tummy Trumpet
Device."

Doctor Glenda used the Tummy Trumpet to listen to what was happening inside the sheep's tummies.

She could hear loud swishing
and swooshing.

"There is a serious amount
of gas in their tummies," said
Doctor Glenda, "and the pressure
is building up."

"I think I know who these sheep belong to," said Nurse Percy. He went to fetch Little Bo Peep. She was really pleased to see her sheep again, but she was also really worried about them.

"There is a dangerous amount of gas in their tummies," said Doctor Glenda.

"For goodness' sake," said Little Bo Peep, "tell Doctor Glenda what happened so she can help you."

The sheep started to cry
because they were so worried.
Rocky began to explain…

"We were only
trying to have some
fun," he said.

"We were going for a
walk with Little Bo Peep,
and when she wasn't
looking, we ran away…"

"...Then we got
to the farmhouse,"
continued Enzo.

"And the door was open, so we went
in. There was a bottle of soda pop on
the table, and we were thirsty after
all that running, so we drank it!"

"But then we were still bored," said Lulu, "so we borrowed the farmer's tractor, just for a little ride."

Old MacDonald was very upset. "I saw them driving my tractor around and around the mulberry bush, and then they crashed and landed in it. That was when I called the ambulance."

"No wonder they feel sick," said Doctor Glenda. "Driving around and around the mulberry bush has shaken up the soda pop in their tummies and caused dangerous gases to build up.

"If the gas doesn't escape, something drastic could happen! There could be internal explosions! Nurse Percy! Get the pink medicine!"

When the sheep saw the pink
medicine they began to cry again.
"Don't worry," said Nurse Percy,
"it doesn't taste that bad."

He gave the sheep one big
spoonful of medicine each.
"The medicine will calm
down their tummies and allow
the gas to escape out of their
bottoms," said Nurse Percy.

The medicine started
to work and the gas
escaped out of the
sheep's bottoms
with a very loud
trumpeting noise!

The sheep felt a lot better.

Nurse Percy had a talk with them. "It is okay to have fun, but it is not okay to run away or go into people's houses and drink their soda pop."

"And stealing
tractors is really,
really naughty."

"You will have to pay for the soda pop out of your pocket money," said Little Bo Peep. The sheep agreed.

Old MacDonald said he
wouldn't call the police if the
sheep promised never to do
anything like
that again. The
sheep promised.

"I can never thank you enough,"
said Little Bo Peep, "I know they
are naughty, but they are still my
sheep, and I love them."

"All in a day's work," said Doctor Glenda. "All in a day's work."

Thanks to Doctor Glenda and her team, the sheep were fine. Little Bo Peep took them home with their tails hanging behind them.